Stanton S Mills

Parisian Sketches

And other stories

Stanton S Mills

Parisian Sketches
And other stories

ISBN/EAN: 9783744747523

Printed in Europe, USA, Canada, Australia, Japan

Cover: Foto ©Andreas Hilbeck / pixelio.de

More available books at **www.hansebooks.com**

PARISIAN

SKETCHES,

AND OTHER STORIES.

———

BY STANTON S. MILLS,

Author of "Love vs. Money," "Church Sociables," "The Pretty Soubrette," "What People Think of Us, "The Heart Bowed Down," Etc.

———

ST. LOUIS, MO.:
FRANK L. SEAVER, PUBLISHER.
1879.

PREFACE.

To write a book is one thing; to sell it is another. And as far as literature of every description is concerned, I unhesitantly assert that it requires a great deal more talent, more perseverance, and more cheek to accomplish the latter than it does the former, public opinion to the contrary notwithstanding.

With especial reference to *amateur* literature it will be readily admitted, by all who have tested it, that this theory is eminently a practical one ; and fully recognizing this fact I am conscious of a feeling, in the publication of "Parisian Sketches" in book form, that the work will fail as a bonanza of wealth or fame. This result, however, is robbed of half its terror when it is remembered that my ambitions are more for a compilation of my works, for my friends and myself, than for any interest which the amateur public might manifest.

Probably no one, into whose hands this volume may fall, will be more impressed with its failings than the author himself, who, realizing his chief error to be in an endeavor to write of that which he knows absolutely nothing, can only offer the apology that the man who is not familiar with your subject will never see your faults. Hence critics can do no less than grant me that lenientcy bestowed on many others who have taken the same liberty as

STANTON S. MILLS.

PARISIAN SKETCHES.

ALLEN ATHERTON'S RECEIPT.

Paris was never before so thronged with Americans as during the year 1873. The hotels were densely packed with foreign visitors attracted thither by the pomp and splendor of this beautiful and dangerous metropolis. Among others from New York were Allen Atherton and Guy Rodman, the former a junior member of a large mercantile establishment of that city, a young man of probably twenty-five years, not particularly handsome, but accomplished, pleasing and gentlemanly in every particular; a most highly esteemed member of society, and considered an excellent example of those sterling qualities, sound judgement and good sense. They were on a pleasure seeking tour, where away from business, they could, for a time, doff the mantle, Wall street care and anxiety, and enjoy the excitement of a season on the continent, consequently in a short time after their arrival at Liverpool they were among the guests located at the Hotel DeChambri, Paris.

A few weeks after this latter event, young Atherton and Rodman were promenading the grand balcony of the hotel, each absorbed in noting the magnificent toilets and beauties of fashion centered in that wealthy throng, when a lady, evidently of French parentage, a most lovely, *petite* and saucy little creature as ever existed, withdrew her delicate jeweled hand from the arm of the gentleman, with whome she was walking, and turning to Allan, smilingly said:

"Monsieur Atherton, 'Giralfie-Giralfia' has perfectly bewitched me and endeavor as I will I utterly fail to impress papa with the slightest degree of enthusiasm, and for an hour I have been trying in vain to convince him that if he should only hear M'lle Duchatel he would return home in extacies."

"You have never heard the opera then, Monsieur DeVarville," observed Atherton, as M'lle unfastening a flower from her hair, placed it in the button hole of his coat.

"Thanks," continued Allan, as he turned to the beauty at his side, "I shall consider this an acceptance to my intended proposal to visit the opera to-night. What say you?"

"With all my heart; then papa prepare
to hear a fresh budget of compliments on
the morrow of M'lle Duchatel, for I am
confident Monsieur Atherton will prove
as great an admirer of her as I."

Rodman and Monsieur DeVarville had
by this time began an animated discus-
sion of the merits of France and America.
Atherton's quick eye saw an opportunity
to gain a delightful promenade with the
vivacious M'lle, who, in the few weeks of
their acquaintance, had so woven the web
of love around his heart, that, struggle as
he would, he found himself powerless to
break asunder its fibers, gave her his arm
and they passed into the parlors.

The opera over, Allan and his beautiful
companion were soon seated in their carriage, being driven slowly homewards.
As the beams of the shinning moon fell
on M'lle DeVarville's countenance, im-

parting a most facinating appearance to her dark, winsome features, she seemed a perfect angel to poor Atherton who silently sat admiring her beauty. With a rippling laugh M'lle DeVarville broke the stillness, saying:

Monsieur Atherton appears unusually melancholy to-night; has he also lost his heart to the handsome prima donna?"

Atherton looked up and gazing into the depths of her lustrous eyes replied.

"No, Pauline, I must call you that, but you are the theif. This visit to the opera was but a ruse of mine to secure an opportunity of telling you how dear you have become to me, in short to ask you to be my wife."

There was no murmuring of undying affection, no falling on his knees and vowing life was chaos without her, no foolish stage nonsense in Allan Atherton's proposal, but a straight, honest and manly assertion.

How tenderly he took her little hand in his and anxiously awaited her reply.

His request had not the slightest effect on her for in a most aggravating manner she gave him her answer.

"Why, Monsieur Atherton, I like and esteem you as deeply as I do or ever can love any one and I would as soon become the wife of you as another; but papa, what will he say? Will you ask him? And to console you, you dear, good fellow, I hope he will consent."

"Nothing would please me better," Allan fervently responded.

"Don't, for pity's sake, ask him unless he is in a good humor, for of late he has been terribly vexed at something."

"I will take good care not to anger him."

On their arrival at the hotel they were met in the parlor by Ninette, M'lle De Varville's waiting maid, who while removing the elegant opera cloak of her mistress succeeded in placing a note in Atherton's hand with a glance that clearly signified the secrecy desired. In a few momonts he bade them *au revoir* and retired to his own apartments where he took occasion to peruse the note, the contents of which aroused a train of curious thoughts in his mind.

"MONSIEUR ATHERTON.—You are too good, too noble, and too generous to be permitted to go on loving M'lle as you do. You will regret it one day for she is unworthy of you and seeks only your fortune."

There was no signature, but Atherton knew Ninette's writing too well to doubt who the author was, and the following day he asked her to explain. She could or would not reveal anything farther than

she had in the letter. A secret convic-
tion, however, led him to believe the girl
foolish enough to construe the little compliments and attentions he frequently
paid her in a far different meaning from
the one intended. He acknowledged to
himself that he had acted unwisely in
flattering Ninette's beauty. The more
he thought of her singular conduct the
more he regreted his hasty proposal to
M'lle, and had it not been for his strict
principles of honor he might have taken
steps to have broken off the engagement.
At any rate he half wished it had been
Ninette instead of Pauline. "Ah! well,"
he thought, "if Ninette has fallen in love
with me it is my own fault, not hers," and
he came to the conclusion that it was her
jeatously which prompted the writing of
the letter and consequently put no confidence in its warning.

With a grave forboding of evil Allan presented himself, the following day, before M. DeVarville, and asked his consent to the marriage.

"What! Would you marry the daughter of a bankrupt? I am hourly expecting the intelligence of our downfall, and unless aid from some source arrives soon, we are ruined. Already I am preparing to depart for Marseilles, and, upon my arrival there expect to find myself without a franc in the world. Now, sir, you understand my position. Do you still wish to marry my daughter?"

Instantly Atherton's mind called up the the words of Ninette, but the man appeared so earnest, he at once dispelled his thoughts. Here was a chance for him to show his love for Pauline by assisting her father in his financial distress and then secure his approval of their marriage.

"What are your liabilities?"

"Our resources are equal to our indebt-
edness, if it comes to that. Our assign-
ment, my partner informs me, will be
made in favor of a London firm, for twenty thousand francs, which must be paid
in three days."

"Can you not borrow?"

"Our friends are as much in need of
money as ourselves, so hope in that direction is useless."

Allan hesitated a moment and then
said :

"I will advance you the sum and your
daughter shall be my receipt. I do this,
not as an inducement to gain your consent
to our marriage but to show my love for
Pauline by assisting you in your present
embarrassment."

"I leave to-night for Marseilles. Give
me the checks for that amount, and in

thirty days it shall be returned with interest, and as to Pauline, gain her consent and you have mine."

Allen immediately drew a check for the
twenty thousand francs, and handed it to
Monsieur DeVarville, who, with all the
flourish of a true born frenchman, thanked him over and over again.

Atherton was the happiest man in existence for the few following days, but
his happiness had a sudden termination
on glancing over the contents of a hasty
letter left by M'lle DeVarville, who, before Ninette really knew what was transpiring, packed her trunks, and announc-
ed her determination of visiting her papa.

"MONSIEUR ATHERTON.—Papa has sent for me.
Allow me to prescribe a remedy for your wound-
ed heart and purse, for you will never see dear
papa or myself again. Marry Ninette, for she
loves you with all her dear little heart and will
prove a more valuable receipt for your twenty
thousand francs, than myself. Content yourself

with knowing that you are not the first American who has fallen a victim to the beauty of
                    PAULINE DEVARVILLE.''

Atherton, like the cool business man he
was, folded the letter and laid it away.
Ninette's bright eyes opened with sur-
prise and astonishment when he informed
her that she had lost her mistress through
him.

"She has gone to her *papa*," with a bitter emphasis on the word papa, "and will
never return   She also leaves you as my
receipt for twenty thousand francs loaned
her dear papa a few days since,   In other
words she requests me to marry you.
which I will only be too happy to do, for
I know you love me for myself and not
for my money."

Ninette, in her gentle, child-like manner consented and ere the fortnight ex-
pired, Atherton and his beautiful little
bride, accompanied by their faithful

Rodman, who by Allen's experience had vowed eternal allegiance to celibacy, were on their way to Baden-Baden.

New York society, a few months later, was surprised to learn that Mr. Atherton was expected home soon, and that he was bringing with him a bride, which fact seemed to have a depressing tendency in the matrimonial market of what is called "good society."

M'LLE VANDORE.

A PARISIAN SKETCH.

A lovely little creature whose sparkling laughing eyes and sweet, winsome smile greets you as you pass. A musical voice, in a pleading, modest manner, asks: " Would Monsieur like some flowers ? "

The Rue De Orm presents a perpetual scene of commotion, and to the eye of strangers, proves a wonderful source of thought and study. Here from the dawning of one morn to the bright rays of another, appear the thousand different phases of a life spent in that beautiful and dangerous French metropolis, Paris. Style, luxury and elegance are there beheld mingling in the vast throng of people with adversity, poverty and beggary. Here the tattered ·and ragged populace jostle their way among fashion, wealth and nobility.

The pretty flower girl (we never heard of a flower girl that was not pretty) who is daily and until the closing of operas, banquettes, feasts and public amusements, late at night to be seen, waiting, her lap full of tulips, jessamines, marigolds, in fact all American flowers, and often standing on the huge stone steps leading to the grand entrance of the Theatre Royal is the florist of all American visitors

Young Neville, the son of a wealthly banker, doing business in a thriving city of New York, was enjoying his first season on the continent, and by his frequent visits to M'lle Vandore for flowers, had discovered in this simple, childlike girl, a person witty, well educated and refined to a marked degree. He it was to whom she addressed the words:

" Would Monsieur, like some flowers ? "

Purchasing a pale white rose with a dainty leaf attached, he fastened it to the lapel of his coat, and passed into the lobby of the Theatre, thence to his box.

The curtain had just gone down on the fourth act of that beautiful French drama, "The Marble Heart," when Neville, feeling fatigued, rose from his seat and leisurly strolled into the *salon*. The night was quite warm and the many cool, shady seats in the brilliantly lighted garden at the rear, was a great temptation. He passed out and finding a vacant seat at the lower end of the garden near the great iron gateway which formed an exit to the Rue La Paris, he sank lazily into it. Scarcely had he seated himself when the gate was thrown suddenly open and M'lle Vandore, in a complete state of exhaustion, tottered through and sank helplessly at his feet, gasping : "Oh, Monsieur, you will not let them harm me I know!"

"Why, poor child, what has happened," asked Neville as he handed her a glass of water from the beautiful fountain at his side.

"I have been so frightened by some bad, cruel men who sought to rob me of my few francs. They pretended to be ill, and came to me as I was waiting for the Theatre to close, and asked for money. I replied that I had but little and needed that worse than they, whereupon one of them grasped me by the waist and endeavored to stop my calling for assistance by placing a cloth over my mouth. With a super-human effort I succeeded in freeing myself from his hold and fled. They followed me to the gateway there, then suddenly stopped."

She seemed greatly excited and could with difficulty relate the particulars of her escape.

"You are safe now, and if you will permit me I will gladly escort you to your home."

"Monsieur is very kind, and we will go at once."

As they passed from Rue La Paris to Rue de Orm they came suddenly upon two men standing on the corner of the street. At the sight of them the girl tremblingly whispered:

"Those are the men."

Neville turned, and, by the light of the dimly shining street lamp could see their faces, which were perfect types of roughs and villians.

The girl directed the way, and from

street to street they passed until Neville found himself in a quarter of Paris he had never before visited. At last they enter a dismal appearing street, or rather alley, devoid of pavements or lamps. Here the darkness became so intense he was unable to discern the way a yard before. He began to experience a keen sense of uneasiness and a suspicion took possession of his mind that he was being led into a trap. Before his thoughts were fairly clear he suddenly felt his arms pinioned to his side by a rope being thrown over his head, and the gleam of a revolver flashed in the darkness, while a hoarse voice hissed in his ear:

"Not one word! Make the slightest noise and you are a dead man."

Not daring to utter a sound, Neville turned to see what effect this remarkable occurrence had on M'lle Vandore. She was no where to be seen, and he was alone in the hands of men whom he well knew would take his life should he breathe aloud. They bound and blind folded him, then the trio moved a short distance and Neville was placed in a carriage; after a drive of a few moment, during which time not a word was spoken by the occupants, the vehicle stopped and they alighted. Here Neville was taken into a rear room of a low, obscure building and the bandage, covering his eyes, removed. Glancing first about the the room he beheld a neat and plainly furnished apartment. The two men, who until now were disguised, removed their masks, and, to Neville's utter astonishment, he immediately recognized them to be the men from whom he had but a short time before rescued the handsome flower-girl. Neville waited for them to break the silence.

"Can you conceive our object in thus bringing you here, Monsuire ?"

"I confess that I am unable."

"Monsieur, you are rich, and we are poor. We have taken this method of obtaining what valuables you posess. Your money is our object, not your life. We must have one or both. If you consent to deliver to us the wealth you now carry, you shall, within the hour be a free man; refuse, and you will never see the rising of to-morrow's sun. Consider our proposition well."

"What little I have at present you are welcome to on those conditions," was Neville's decision. What else could he do. He fully realized how useless it would be to resist.

"Will you tell me if M'lle Vandore is an accomplish of yours," he continued.

"We commit no one but ourselves. She

is far more capable of taking care of herself, than you are of your wealth," replied the man evasively.

"I have a suspicion that her part of these proceedings were bnt a ruse to lead me into your path. Here are the only articles of value, together with what money I have about my person," said Neville as he handed the man his wallet, watch and jewels, with as much self-possession as though he was paying a just and honest debt.

"You are wise. We will once more blind-fold you and lead you to the entrance of Rue De Orm, when you will be at liberty to remove the covering from your eyes, which will require some time, during which we shall make good our escape. Your life depends upon your conduct. The first attempt to attract attention will meet with death."

In a few moments they had left the house. After walking a great distance the men suddenly left his side, one saying:

"This is Rue De Orm."

Neville could not determine, so noislessly did they glide away, the direction they took, and by the time he had removed the cloth from his eyes, they were far beyond the hopes of ever seeing them.

The following evening Neville wended his steps to the Theatre Royal, expecting to find M'lle Vandore at her usual post. She was missing. Then it was he became fully convinced that he had fallen a victime to one of the many ingenious devices, only to be invented by a Frenchman, for robbing foreigners.

On returning to the hotel where he was stopping, Neville narrated his adventures of the foregoing night to the proprietor, a genial and whole-souled Frenchman, and asked his opinion.

"My dear fellow," playfully remarked the landlord, "you will look in vain for the beautiful florist. It is as plain as the nose on your handsome face. Her fleeing to you for protection was but a ruse to get you to offer yourself as an escort, and you swallowed the bait, like the innocent American you are, hook and all, thus walking into a cleverly planned strategem with its chief opperator. It is the same old story, American galantry and French cunning.

"I have learned a lesson that I will never forget at any rate," observed Neville as he passed into the *salon.*

The hotel proprietor was right. Neville saw no more of M'lle Vandore, although he searched the great city from one end to the other.

THE SPECTER OF CHATEAU DeCOURCEY.

A PARISIAN SKETCH,

ONE never becomes thoroughly acquainted with the mysteries and miseries of Parisian Life until by some fortunate combination of circumstances he drifts into the newspaper fraternity. Here he he finds an occupation which leads him through the highways and byways; gives him a deeper insight to the hidden and public lives of Parisians, the chief elements of which he soon discovers to be a curious mixture of trickery, romance and fashion, than is obtainable in any any other calling he may adopt. It is somewhat amusing to observe the pres-

ence of these characteristics of the genuine Frenchman wherever one may go.
The rag-picker and the nobleman have
alike a fondness for romance, trickery and
fashion. Tell to the genuine Parisian a
tale of romance, sprinkled with a trifle
love and a vast amount of knavery, and
you will have pleased his fancy beyond
anything else you could have done for
him, unless it be to introduce him to your
wife, especially should she happen to be a
charmingly handsome woman. The newspaper reporter is no exception to the av-
erage Parisian, and equally delights in
detailing the particulars of a little romantic episode, with his readers in a perusal
of them. How eagerly he watches the
result of any mysterious chain of events
which come under his observation, in
hopes of obtaining a rare treat for his
readers, in the shape of some startling

developments concerning a newly discovered bit of romance.

The Specter of Chateau DeCourcy was
a mystery that puzzled all Paris and perhaps would have remained a profound one
to the present time, had it not been for
Achile Duval, a reporter for the ———,
who discovered and published an account,
toned and polished to an extremely
French degree, of the mysterious Specter.

Not many years ago there came to Paris
an apparently very wealthy and positive-
ly very eccentric Frenchman, named De-
Courcy, who purchased a lovely little vil-
la at the outskirts of the city, and called
it "Chateau DeCourcy." He brought with
him an only and accomplished daughter,
whose extreme beauty and devotion to
her aged father excited no little curiosity.
From the moment of their advent the
Chateau became enveloped in a shroud of

mystery, inasmuch as no one knew from whence Monsieur and M'lle DeCourcy came, and the most rigid efforts to discover the slightest particulars of their past history proved futile. They made no acquaintances and obstinately refused to mingle in any society whatever. With the exception of a few servants they lived all alone, and were rarely seen save when when driving along the Boulevards, always together. No wonder the Parisian appetite for romance found in these strange people excellent subjects for a vast amount of gossip.

A year went by and all Paris still wondered more and more who M. and M'lle DeCourcy were.

This formed the first part of Achille Duval's tale of romance. The one which followed, terrible as it was, still left Paris in, if possible, a deeper wonderment.

One beautiful morning the Chateau, usually so calm and quiet, presented a scene of excitement never to be forgotten. The servants were hurrying to and fro in a terrible state of agitation. Passers-by were stopped and conducted into the house, soon emerging with awe stricken and terrified countenances, telling only too plainly that something dreadful had occurred. In a few hours all Paris was made acquainted with the particulars of the great tragedy at the Chateau.

Pale as death Mons. DeCourcy slowly paced the hallway, while from his eyes was emitted that peculiar gleam which betrays a dethroned reason. He seemed utterly unconscious of what was transpiring around him, paying not the least attention to the many persons who stopped to watch his singular actions. In a small but elegantly furnished boudoir, a piti-

ful sight met the eye. Lying, on the soft
brussels carpet, with the paleness of death
on her beautifnl countenance, was M'lle
DeCourdy, her long, dark hair falling
loosely about her fair, white shoulders.
Death had accomplished its work quietly
and quickly.

The servants were questioned and the
terrible life secret of Mons. and M'lle De-
Courcy revealed. It was· a long story
which they had gathered, little by little,
from conversations with their master and
mistress. For years Monsieur DeCourcy
had been the victim of a mild and harm-
less state of insanity, during which he had
conceived the singular idea that he and
M'lle were proof against the poisionous
effects of all deadly drugs, and had re-
peatedly endeavored to illustrate to his
daughter that they could not die, by at-
tempting to induce her to drink of various

mixtures he would prepare. How carefully had the poor girl guarded the secret of her father's insanity, only to become the victim of a cruel, untimely death at his hands. The usual ceremonies of the law were gone through with and M'lle DeCourcy quietly laid to rest, while her father, adjudged insame, was sent to an asylum at Marseilles. Thus the second part of Achile Duval's novel was complete.

Another year had passed and the Chateau DeCourcy, through the agency of an administrator had passed into the hands of new tenants, and with then came another and a deeper mystery. "Surely," said Duval, in one of his articles, "the Chateau was doomed to become a continual scene of wonderment to the end of its existence." Mons. Sartory, the new occupant of the Chateau, used every endeavor to hush the whisperings that were being indulged concerning the "Specter of Chateau De Courcy," but without avail. In a few weeks after his arrival all Paris was teeming with excitement over the pale, sad face that nightly appeared at the window of poor M'lle DeCourcy's boudoir. The apartment was never occupied thereafter, and Mons. Sartorys, superstitious as he was, would permit no effort to be made towards discovering the cause of the strange apparation, placing the utmost confidence in the theory that it was the spirit of the ill-fated girl. On one or two occasions he had been prevailed upon to allow persons to occupy the chamber over night, in hopes of ascertaining some clue to the mystery. No one appeared able to arrive at any definite conclusions other than that the apparition seemed to appear and disappear leaving no trace of

its entrance or exit,   Achile Duval, vexed at the unsuccessful efforts of others,
determined to visit the Chateau, and there
remain until he could explain to all Paris
the true cause of their foolish superstition.
Mons. Sartorys received him courteously
and offered every assistance in his power,
but ventured to remark that it was a haz-
ardous undertaking, and feared would ter-
minate with no more satisfactory results
than others had achieved.   Achile was
shown through the Chateau, and made acquainted with Mme. and M'lle Sartorys,
the latter being a beautiful neice of the
courteous Frenchman.   M'lle, unlike her
guardians, seemed pleased at Duval's determination, and expressed a sanguine
hope that his mission would prove a tri-
umphant one.

Every preparation being perfected,
Achile bid all a reluctant good-night, and

retired to the mysterious room. Only
partially disrobing, he lay down to watch
and wait the appearance of the spectre.
The moon shown brightly, and as its rays
came through the window he could distinctly see every object in the room. How
long he waited he could not tell; for becoming weary and tired, he at last sank
into a slight slumber, only to be awaken-
en by the rushing of a cold, damp gust of
wind through the room. The moon had
sank below the horizon and the Chateau
was in total darkness. He felt certain
that the door or some of the windows to
apartment were open, and on examina-
tion, to his utter astonishment, he found
that the door, which he had so carefully
locked, was indeed open. How hard he
endeavored to persuade himself that he
was not frightened, and courageously he
again closed the door, this time placing

a chair in such a position, that it would be impossible to open the door without causing a crash from the chair falling to the floor. Again he lay down, this time with a determination to allow nothing to escape him unnoticed. With all his efforts to keep his eyes open he experienced, as time flew by, and no appearance of the specter, a sense of drowsiness creeping over him; and ere he was aware of it he had fallen into a broken sleep. With a start he awoke to find *the chair removed and the door again standing wide open.* If he was frightened before, he was doubly so now. With a face as pale as death and trembling like an aspen leaf, he closed the door. What should he do? His first impulse was to arouse the family, but upon a second consideration he determined not to do so. He had came there for the purpose of meeting the dreaded spectre

face to face, and he would fulfill his mission come what might; and with this re-
solve he drew a chair to the window,
threw up the sash, and concluded to pass
the remainder of the night watching the
exterior instead of the interior of the
building. For a long time he sat watching and thinking, endeavoring to account
for the mysterious opening of the door,
when suddenly he became conscious of a
dull red light filling the room, and then
upon the wall before him he beheld a
sight which caused his heart to beat wildly with terror; he tried to speak, but his
tongue seemed paralyzed; he made an
effort to move, but found it impossible.
Through an aperture in the wall he could
distinctly see the hand and arm of a hu-
man being, evidently a woman, for they
were of exquisite mould, white as marble;
and the small tapering fingers were busy

removing the panels of a secret door, till a space was vacant sufficient to admit the body. Slowly and cautiously the apparition came through the opening, bearing in her hand a beautiful lamp, which, when its red glare shone in Duval's face, revealed to him the. countenance of the "Spectre of Chateau De Courcy."   To say Achile was astonished seems foolish; he was completely dumbfounded; for, with her eyes still closed in sleep, and her fair white shoulders hid by a mass of long shining hair, *there before him stood M'lle Sartorys,* her face as white as the snowy night clothes she was clad in. With a noiseless step she advanced to the door and removed the chair, then turning the key she gently swung the door open. Duval deemed it prudent to make no movement towards awakening the fair sleeper, and permitted her to leave the

room unmolested, which she did by means
of the secret door in the wall. Carefully
the unconscious girl replaced the panels,
and all was again as still as death.

Morning came at last, and how joyful-
ly Achile welcomed its first bright rays.
He had accomplished what had been considered impossible, but at what a cost!
He was thoroughly exhausted and very
weak from excitement and fright. At the
breakfast table he met M'lle Sartorys,
who, in answer to his inquiry, informed
him that she had never rested better. He
thought it best to keep his knowledge of
her sleep-walking a secret, until it should
be made known through the columns of
the next morning's paper; and when M.
Sartorys asked what his success was, he
merely replied that he had saw no spectre.

The particulars were soon published,
and Duval became the lion of the hour.

The problem was solved at last and he had done it. Paris was satisfied, Mons. and Mme. Sartorys were nonplussed, Mll'e was at a loss to comppehend its meaning, and Achile's romance was ended, and with it the excitement over the "Spectre of Chateau DeCourcy."

AT THE DOOR OF A CONVENT.

A PARISIAN SKETCH.

A lovely face. The expression of tenderness, beaming from a pair of large blue eyes, caused George Lesparre's heart to throb wildly with admiration. Vainly he endeavored to persuade himself into the belief that he only admired the beauty of the face and not the person herself. He flattered himself that he was too wise to ever imagine Lucille Chandoce, beautiful, accomplished and heiress to a world of wealth, ever becoming foolish enough to forget her station in life and bestow her love upon a poor artist, far beneath her in rank and intellect. "No, not intellect," he argued with himself. "I am certain she possesses no more of what the world pleases to call learning than myself." But rank rendered impassable the gulf between them, and as he permitted his deep, dark eyes to wander toward her own, he felt the folly of ever aspiring to think of her as the wife of a toiling, struggling artist with nothing in the world but an education calculated to create hopes and expectancies impossible ever to realize.

The scene was one of rare beauty, such as only Parisians delight to dazzle the eye with, and as George Lespare's glance beheld the brilliantly lighted parlors of Monsieur Chandoce's magnificent mansion, where mingled the grandeur and elegance of a Parisian gathering, he wondered why he was permitted to be present. However unworthy he had seemed

of Lucille before he could but think, as
he saw her courted and admired by all'
around her, how far above him she was.
He dared not approach her and beg the
indulgence of a mazourka as others did,
but quietly stole away into a deserted
corner of the drawing room and endeavored to concentrate his thoughts in a volume of Dumas. How utterly incapable
of doing aught but eagerly watch the
sweet face of Lucille, as she promenaded
the hallway before him. He began to experience keenly a feeling that his reserve
and silence were being noticed by the
guests, and he wished a thousand times
that he could frame an excuse that he
might leave the house.

George Lesparre was a man upon whom
nature had bestowed that faculty, one
rarely encounters, of sincerity in every
word uttered and every thought of his

mind. Giddyness and hypocracy could never be traced in the slightest action of his life. When he spoke people knew he was in earnest. Lucille had just tinge enough of sentiment in her nature to recognize in these qualifications a man whose esteem, if once gained could never be altered, come what would. She knew when he told a woman he loved her it was with a love constant as the changing of hours into days, days into years, and years into eternity, and, as she thought of these things, she saw how, a contrast with the many admirers around her, revealed his invaluable worth as a man and a friend. Cold and distant, as he always seemed to her, she was learning to love him, for the more she saw of him, the more she found many things to admire in his upright, honest character.

"Monsieur Lesparre, you seem lonely

here, all by yourself," quietly spoke Lucille, as she ventured into the drawing
room. He looked slowly up, with a smile
which Lucille thought more of sadness
than pleasure.

"I should not feel at home in there, and
I do here by myself," and he lowered his
eyes to the book again.

Lucille waited some moments for him
to speak again and when the silence was
becoming awkward she said pleasantly:

"I am tired of waltzing and have come
to you for a stroll in the conservatory,
thinking perhaps I might dispel your
lonliness. Will you accompany me?"

"With pleasure," and replacing the book
with a carefulness that pleased Lucille he
offered her his. arm and they passed out
into the conservatory.

"Why do you so persistently avoid me,
Monsieur," asked Lucille, when alone.

He stopped, withdrew her hand from his arm, and, casting a look full of earnestness into her troubled face, said:

"Ah, M'llle, you should have asked why I am unable to make myself agreeable as you wish. I will tell you. I cannot play the part of a hypocrite and compliment the frivolity and vanity with which I am surrounded, thus rendering me an object of dislike."

"Monsieur Lesparre, I abhor flattery and false compliments even as you, but for the sake of society I am constrained to listen to it. Surely, whatever your aversion to society may be, it should be no excuse for your indifference towards me."

Something like a sound of sadness and reproach seemed to characterize her words, and the drooping head and trembling voice betrayed her thoughts too well.

Lesparre noticed it and in his heart he thanked her. When he replied he could not conceal the thoughts which filled his mind, and passionately told her all.

"Lucille, I love you. That is why I avoid you; and I dared not speak for fear of betraying myself. I know the folly of loving you, and fully understand the great difference of our positions. I know I cannot please you with my sober, silent ways, therefore I am content to see and admire you without the privilege of telling you of my admiration.

"Oh! Monsieur. I am so glad you have spoken of this; it gives me a pretext for telling you how much more I value your nobleness of mind than the light, trifling customs of society, as does every woman with one spark of honesty in her nature."

"And yet she would refuse the love of such a man!" rapidly responded Lesparre.

as he leaned toward her to note the effect of his words. She raised her head and looked straight at him for the first time and firmly said:

"Never, if she loved him!"

"Dare I hope, then, that you would not refuse to listen to me if I would ask you to become my wife. Can I think you would overlook my poverty and grant me one word of encouragement. Speak, Lucille, and tell me."

He trembled like an aspen when she looked up again, this time her face pale, and her voice low and quivering, as she answered:

"George Lesparre, my father would rather see me shut forever within the walls of a convent than the wife of a poor man, but for all that I love you, for I know you are good, generous and kind. I *will* marry you in spite of my father's

remonstrances, if you will brave the con-
sequences with me."

The world never before seemed half so
bright to George Lesparre, as when he
leaned tenderly down and pressed a sweet
passionate kiss upon Lucille's white hand.
Poor Girl! She little thought of the misery and sorrow she was bringing upon
herself. She had but one thought—her
love for George—and in that she could be
happy anywhere.

With a heart sad and sorrowful, George
listened to M. Chandoce's kind, sympa-
thetic refusal of his daughter's hand.

"It cannot be, George. Much as I esteem and regard you, I could never think
of Lucille becoming your wife. You may,
as you say, love her, and love may be
very pleasant, but money is omnipotent,
and therefore indispensable," and George
knew how true his words were. "It is

better you go away for a time to Italy, or
Switzerland, or England, where, in the
pursuit of your profession, you will soon
learn to think of Lucille as only a friend."

"Oh! Monsieur, I could never do that.
It would look too much like I had regretted my action and was eager to shut Lucille forever from my mind."

But Monsieur Chandoce was inexorable,
and, at last, when George quit the house,
he felt that Lucille was farther from him
than ever.

For two days Lucille waited and watch-
ed for the coming of George with an anxiety that almost made her ill, and still he
did not come to tell her to hope one.   M.
Chandoce, perceiving her solicitude, endeavored te urge her to believe that
George, seeing the error of his conduct,
had departed for England where he could
drive the thoughts of herself from his

mind. She tried hard not to think him so cruel and false, but when one evening there came a letter from him she doubted no longer.

"LUCILLE.—By the time you will have received this I shall be far away. I have realized before it was too late, how unsuited we are to each other, and I quit Paris forever to-night, that I might aid you in forgetting one who could only . make your life a miserable one.

Regretfully, GEORGE.

It was all over now. Henceforth the name of George Lespare, a few hours before so dear, was but the name of an utter stranger whom she could meet at any moment and dispel from her mind the next. These were Lucille's thoughts as she threw the fragments of the letter, which had brought so much pain and sorrow to her heart, into the fire.

Alone in his room George Lesparre was suffering the pangs of a bitter, bitter life; the past, dark and mournful, haunting him like a dream, the future foretold naught but distress. His head was bowed and in his hand he clasped a letter, murmuring, as he gazed upon it, not words of censure but words of compassion and pity. Lucille was false to him, but he loved her deeply and devotedly, knowing as he did that she was lost to him forever.

"Why did I allow myself to speak? I could have lived on in happiness if I had never told her how I loved her. I will go away as she requests, and wait till time effaces the memory of her falseness."

In one short week he had left Paris, the scene of the happiest and the saddest moments of his life. He wrote Lucille a long, tender letter forgiving her and asking that he be remembered when, as the years flew past, she was the happy wife of one whom she could love more than she had him.

*   *   *   *   *   *

Along the almost deserted Rue St. Ma-
ry walked George Lesparre, once more in
Paris, after an absence of two years
abroad; long and weary years to him;
years of suffering to Lucille. And now
he has returned because way down in his
heart was a longing to see Lucille, which,
try as he would, he could not resist. The
silence and solemnity of the night were
only broken by the deep toned bell of the
grand Cathedral of St. Peter as it rang
out the hour. A moment more and the
great organ of the Cathedral was heard.
How solemn the music sounded, as he listened to the strains of the Sonata from
"Martha." Some strange presentament
seemed to guide his footsteps to the
church where he had often been with Lucille, and urged him to enter. Slowly he
ascends the steps and enters. The sight

which greets him was one he never can forget. It seemed to stop the pulsations of his heart. His head grew dizzy and the room appeared to swim before his eyes. There before the altar, her face pale as death, robed in garments white as the snow covered ground without, stood Lucille Chandoce. What did it all mean. Alas! the appearance of the Bishop told him too well. It was the beginning of a ceremony which would shut Lucille forever from the world. A ceremony that would close before her the doors of liberty and happiness. Poor Lucille! Sick at heart with herself and all around her she was soon to be ushered within the iron walls of a convent.

For a moment George stood gazing at the scene before him, and then in a voice tremulous with emotion he speaks, scarcely knowing why he does so, while the eyes of all within the church were turned towards him.

"May heaven bless you, Lucille, false as you have been to me."

The voice, the face of one, whom, for two years she had striven to forget, brought back the memory of the moments when hè had told her how he loved her. Her brain was whirling; the very air seemed to stifle her, and with a low moan of anguish Lucille sank helpless and miserable to the floor.

Tenderiy they placed her in her carriage anc conveyed her to her home.

For a long time Lucille lay unconscieus and when at last she slowly opened her eyes the physician forbade any one but the nurse entering the room.

˙ George came every day to inquire after her, bringing with him flowers, books, and many other things to aid her in passing the weary hours away How his heart bounded when they told him he could see Lucille. He trembled in every limb as he entered the room. Their eyes met and looked the love that neither could speak. Gently he kissed her as she looked up with a smile full of love and constancy.

"But, Lucille," said George, when their first greeting was over, "why did you send me this cruel letter?"

"Oh! George, I never penned that letter. I could not be so false as that. Even when your letter came telling me you could never see me again, I forgave you, for I still loved you."

"Never penned that letter?" asked Lesparre, in astonishment. "Then there must be some terrible misunderstanding ——"

He was interrupted by the entrance of M. Chandoce, who said :

"I can explain all. George, I am a scoundrel. It was I who penned those letters which came so near severing your hearts, I was mad enough once to think it best to seperate you and Lucille, and for that purpose the letter which you received was written under my directions. Your reply was treated in like manner ere it reached Lucille. But I have suffered untold misery ever since. I could not be blind to her feelings, and yet I dared not tell her. Lucille, my child, can you forget the past and forgive me?"

"I would do anything in my power to make you happy again, and if forgivness will accomplish it, there's a kiss, dear papa, to seal my pledge that all is forgiven," replied the happy girl, as she seated herself an a ottoman at his feet.

"George," continued Monsieur, "I have wronged you deeply, and I beg your forgiveness also. I will do what I can to atone for that wrong. Give me your hand. I refused you the hand of Lucille; I now revoke that refusal. Take her, and may the sorrow which I brought upon you reap only happiness add contentment.

Another month had flown past when the bells of the old Cathedral St. Peter rang out the glad welcome of a new life for George and Lucille Lesparre, while the sweet tones of "Wedding Bells March" told too truly the story of their happiness.

EDNA SEYMOUR'S MISTAKE.

———

"Dumb jewels, often, in their silent kind,
More than quick words, do move a woman's mind."
SHAKESPEARE.

GOLD! This was the bright and glittering shrine at which beautiful Edna Seymour, obeying the mandates of a fashionable society, in which she moved as the reigning queen, bowed her head in humble worship. Grace, beauty and frivolity found in her a most worthy exponent. A lovely creature whose dark, luminous eyes betrayed a depth of passion so gentle and yet so dangerous. From infancy every thing that heart could desire or money purchase, were lavished upon this fairy-

like being who found in them the value
and power of those great levers of this
world's opinion, wealth, luxury and elegance, and now that the time was fast approaching when she must accept one of
the many applications for her hand in
marriage, she had tutored her mind to regard money as the first consideration of
wedded life.

Proud, haughty and willful, no wonder
her mind shuddered at the possibility of
one day becoming the wife of a penny-
less man. Love, the ruling passion of
some lives, was a stranger to her heart—
a heart of marble—dead to every thing
save *gold*.

Edna was an orphan, and her uncle and
aunt, Sir John and Lady Winthrop, upon
whom she was dependent. always urged
the necessity of a wealthy marriage, pic-
uring to her the sorrowful life spent as

the wife of a commoner. Give up the
many joys and pleasures of her present
home for the toil and care of another?
How her mind revolted. Ah! Edna little dreamed how near was the dawning
of the day when the folly of her life would
appear, never to be forgotten. The great
lesson, which was destined to work a wonderful change in her icy heart was soon
to be learned.

Not more than an hour's ride from the
bussy, bustling, English metropolis, London, the quiet, little parish, called Lawndale, is situated. Lawndale was indeed a
lovely place, and rightly named too. Edna often called it paradise, and truly, with
it magnificent gravel drives, winding here
and there through the trees lining the
mossy banks of a murmuring stream, it
reminded one of that enchanting spot so
beautifully described by Milton. Here

was the home of Sir John Winthrop—
"Winthrop Place" it was called—and ad-
joining, with its grand old estates, stood
Vivan Hall, half hid from view by the
thick foliage of trees forming an avenue,
picturesque and romantic, leading to the
great iron gate fronting the highway.
Vivan Hall was the pride of Lawndale,
and frequently had Edna, in her morning
rambles, stopped to note the beauty and
elegance of its surroundings, always won-
dering if the young heir, when he came
to take posession of his inheritance, would
keep the doors of the grand old building
closed against tourists and visitors as did
his uncle, Sir Mortimer Vivan. Here for
years, hermit-like and alone, save the
presence of a few servants, had Sir Mortimer lived, rarely venturing outside his
lonely room. Suddenly one morning the

news was rung throughout the parish
that the master of Vivan Hall was no
more. It was only too true. In the lonliness of his room Sir Mortimer had quietly passed from earth. The old hall, it was
soon learned, reverted to a nephew, a
stranger to Lawndale, and who, after com-
pleting his studies at one of the English
Universities, would come to his new home
for the first time. This it was that turned the thoughts of beautiful Edna into a
strange current, as she stood gazing
through the trees. Her plotting mind
was busy at work. She was dreaming of
a hope, a hope which sprang from the
great object of her life, that one day she
might become the mistress of Vivan Hall;
the thought sent a thrill of determination
through her mind, and she was slowly
forming a resolution to win the the heir,
cost what it may. True, she had never

seen Walter Vivan, but she cared little
for that. Her nature taught her to love
his money, not himself. She knew well
the power of her facinating beauty, but
she realized not the bitter ending of false
expectations which its blandishments
were fast leading her to.

*　　*　　*　　*　　*　　*

Two months have passed since the death
of Sir Mortimer, and the smiling summer
days slowly fading into autumn, brought
many changes to Vivan Hall. The great,
old-fashioned paneled doors, which for
years had remained closed, were now
thrown open and the warm sunlight steal-
ing in, imparted a bright, genial appearance to the dingy rooms of the old building. Already the servants were busy
making preparations for a grand reception of the new master, and the little
parish seemed to take a renewen interest

in the coming of the young heir, who was coming on a visit to his new home during vacation.

Changes had occurred at Winthrop Place as well. Sir John, Lady Winthrop and Edna, according to custom, had gone to London to spend the Winter season, "for," said Edna, "Lawndale was so lonely during the Holidays."

Edna loved society and at the many brilliant reception parties, where thronged English nobility and fashion, she always seemed the magnet to which they were drawn.

The turning point in Edna's life was drawing nearer and nearer. A fashionable soiree was given at the home of Col. Ellington, a wealthy London banker. Here Edna's beauty became the object of many admiring eyes, for never before had she appeared so lovely. It was a very brilliant assembly and Edna made many new acquaintances, among whom was a friend of Col. Ellington, Arnold Burdette by name, then visiting relatives in London. Cold and distant as Edna had always seemed to every one, she found it impossible to be so with Arnold. From the moment their eyes met they seemed intimate friends, They waltzed together and ever and anon she found herself glancing around half expecting, half hoping he was near. Life's path had suddenly taken a new turning it appeared to her.

The season wore on and still Sir John and his family remained in London. Every opportunity fonnd Edna and Arnold together. One evening as she sat at the piano. idly fingering the keys, Arnold abruptly turned the conversation and in a trembling voice said:

"Edna, for weeks I have been vainly trying to say what I am determined to now. I have come to-night to ask you to be my wife. I am poor as you doubtless-ly know, but bright prospects are before me and with willing hands and you to toil for, our future has no shadow."

Her head was buried in her hands, and a heart, which but a moment before had been so light, was now aching with sorrow. It was a fierce struggle between love and gold with her. In that single sentence "Will you be my wife?" spoken so tenderly came from the almost buried thought of Walter Vivan, and the vow she had made. She loved Arnold Burdette with all her soul and mind, but she loved Vivan Hall better. At last she looked up, the same old haughty, cold look upon her face and with a quivering lip said :

"Arnold, you do not know how it wrings my heart to hear you speak thus. It grieves me worse, if possible, to say it, than you to hear me when I tell you that I can never become your wife. You will think me the incarnation of falseness, caprice and selfishness were I to tell you why. You say you are poor. Look at me now, surrounded with every luxury imaginable. Divest me of these claims to the respect of society and what am I. A person to mocked and spurned. I am dependent on the charities of my uncle and aunt, while you are no better situated. No, Arnold, wealthy marriage is my only hope, aye, it is the object of my life. It is better that we part and learn to forget each other."

"Edna, that is an answer prompted by an avaricious nature, and not by your heart."

"Call it what you may, it is my answer."

"Farewell then. You reject my love because I am poor and not because you do not love me in return. I can read this in your eyes, your smile and your actions. Edna, we may meet again; till then, adieu." He was gone.

Edna half regretted the step she had taken. She could not bear to give up all hopes of Vivan Hall and yet she longed to call Arnold back and at least tell him that she loved him, poor as he was. She arose from the piano and walked to the window, while a feeling of sadness and sorrow began to take posession of her. In vain she endeavored to drive all thoughts of Arnold's pale face from her mind.

The bright spring days were rapidly approaching and the Winthrops were preparing to return to Lawndale.

*   *   *   *   *

Summer had again rolled 'round and Lawndale was anxiously and eagerly awaiting the arrival of Sir Walter to take possession of Vivan Hall. Edna, once so desirous to see the young heir, seemed to have lost all interest in the change which the Hall was soon to undergo. The coming of Walter Vivan had no effect upon her, and when the invitations to attend the reception were received at Winthrop Place, she expressed a desire to remain away.

Lady Winthrop was surprised and urged her to go, and plainly hinted that Sir Walter would probably look for a bride among the assembly. Edna understood the meaning of her aunt's allusion, and suffered herself to be present.

It was a bright moonlight night when

the coachman drove to the gates of Winthrop Place ; and in a few moments Edna, pale, trembling and silent, with Sir John and Lady Winthrop, was on her way to Vivan Hall. The old building was thronged with guests, filling the great corridors. and verandas, and in a few moments Edna was to be presented to the man she had once vowed to win. Why did she, coquettish and merry as she usually was before she knew Arnold Burdette, now remain so silent and reserved? Her face, now as white as the robes she wore, seemed more beautiful and lovely than ever before.

"Miss Seymour, allow me to present to you Sir Walter Vivan, the new master of Vivan Hall. Sir Walter, Miss Seymour."

"*Arnold !*"

"*Edna !*"

The lesson was learned. There before her, with the same look of sadness as on the night she refused his hand, stood Arnold Burdette.

Arnold, or Sir Walter, was the first to speak :

"Edna, we are still friends ; at least, I hope?"

He offered her his arm, as she mechanically responded : "Always friends, if nothing more."

They passed through the throng of people out into the observatory.

" Here we will be unmolested for a few moments, Edna," said Arnold, as he offered her a seat; " and I want to tell you now what I have longed to since that night, the memory of which will ever be as fresh in my mind as I know it will be in yours. The deception I practiced,

while in London, was the result of Col.
Ellington's devices to keeping identity
unknown until I came to Vivan Hall.   It
was perhaps foolish and unwise, but it
taught you to love me for myself and not
for my wealthy position.   I do not censure you for refusing me, believing as you
did that I was a penniless man ; for I, too,
have seen poverty and love go through
this world hand in hand down to a bitter
grave.   Edna, once again I ask you to
take back those words and say that you
will be my wife."

"Can you so forgive me, Arnold, as
to ask that?" was Edna's reply, as tears
filled her eyes.

"Aye, more ; I can forget.   Will you
not recall your words"?

Edna's answer brought a bright joyous
look into the deep blue eyes of Arnold,

while the color came again to Edna's cheeks.

Three months later, Vivan Hall was the scene of another happy gathering when

> "Two souls with but a single thought.
> Two hearts that beat as one."

And Edna was Lady Vivan after all.

In the Art Gallery of Florence, Italy, there hangs a portrait bearing the inscription,

" THE HEART BOWED DOWN."

The portrait is that of a young and beautiful girl, whose sorrowful face rarely fails to attract attention, and excite the sympathy of visitors. The interest awakened in the painting is greatly augmented by reference to the catalogue, and the name of a once promising young artist of America is found appended as the author, whose life seems to have been a

bitter failure ; as the following history of
the work, written by the artist himself,
would indicate. No one has ever been
able to obtain any definite information
concerning the girl referred to, other than
that vouchsafed by the artist. It is sup-
posed, however, that the painting was ex-
ecuted in America and brought to Florence,
together with the accompanying account
of its production, at the dying request of
the unfortunate artist :

"There comes a voice that awakes my soul. It is the
voice of years gone by; they roll before me with their
deeds."—OSSIAN.

Nature's cold, inanimate touch was
fast spreading a mantle of dreariness over
Oak Dale Cemetery, as I stood before its
great iron gate ; peering through the railings, my glances wandered up the road-
way, now strewn with dead and withered
leaves. The once green and verdant for-

est, reaching far away 'till the summits
of its lofty trees seemed to pierce the gray
sky overhead, now presented a view bar-
ren and desolate. Instinctively I closed
my eyes that imagination might again
bring to my mind the memory of sunny
summer days, when, beneath the luxur-
iant foliage, I had wandered, a little
sketch-book as my companion, listening
to the sweet warbling of birds as they
fluttered to and fro among the branches.
But as I looked again the same bleak and
gloomy scene appears. Why could not
nature forsake her duty and leave the
world to enjoy the beauties thus destroyed?
I asked myself, as my hand involuntarily
grasped the gate to swing it open. Alas!
Man and nature seldom harmonize.

Slowly I swung the ponderous gate on
its hinges, and I stood within the enclos-

ure, I paused and shuddered, so impress-
ive was the scene before me. Trees, flowers and shrubbery seemed sharing in the
death sleep of those who had passed away
from earth and were forever laid to rest.
The white marble monuments, staring me
in the face, as I silently passed up the avenue, seemed to tell the story of dear and departed friends, whose last resting place
they marked, that life's autumn had come
too quickly for them.

Seating myself on the base of one of
the many beautiful railings, which adorned
the cemetery, I drew forth my sketch-book
and pencil, while my eyes drank in the
magnificent scenery with which I was
surrounded ; scenery that no artist's hand,
much less my own, could ever hope to
paint. The deep, dark ravine, at the bot-
tom of which a little rill of water trickled,

with its rippling music over its pebbly bed.
Leafless branches, mosses peeping from
out a thick covering of yellow and purple
leaves, flowers dead and dying, clinging
ivy and weeping willows, leaning tenderly
over graves now sunken with age; all
these the artist's brush could paint. But
there was something which even his magic
touch could not produce; something that
would defy his inspiration. He could
never paint the stillnes of Death, which
reigned supreme.

For a few moments I sat in thoughtful
meditation, when I was suddenly aroused
from my reverie by sounds of a footstep,
and the rustle of leaves. Hastily looking
up, I discerned through the trees, the approaching figure of a woman, clad in deep-
est mourning. Ah! thought I, some sor-
rowing friend who had come hither to pay

a silent tribute of respect to the dead. Nearer and nearer she came. Intently gazing at the ground, she hid her face from my view, till she came almost upon me, when, with a startled look, she glanced up. Oh! the look of anguish which she gave me as she passed! How I wish I could paint the sorrow which shone in her eyes. Silently she passed on down the avenue of trees. Stopping near a newly-made grave, she sank upon her knees beside the little mound of clay. Reverentially she clasped her small white hands before her, and turned her face toward heaven. It was the face of a young girl, just budding into womanhood. Tears now filled her eyes, and my whole soul went out in pity for this poor creature, whose sorrow seemed a load too heavy for her young heart. Her lips moved

devoutly in prayer. Some unseen hand
seemed to guide my fingers as I traced
the outlines of her delicate countenance
in the book before me. With a few strokes
of my pencil I caught the expression of
devotion that shone through her tears.
I saw, I saw, I heard nothing, but the object, the object before me, so intensely was
my mind buried in thought of this poor
girl, the image of whose face seemed to
burn itself into my very heart. With the
rapidity of lightning my pencil traced
every feature. I seemed wrapped in a
dream, from which a low moan of anguish
aroused me, and looking up I beheld the
grief-stricken child sink to the ground,
sobbing bitterly, as though her heart was
breaking, while she buried her face in her
hands. Man though I was, I felt the
tears come to my eyes, and as I arose to

shut the sight from me I heard a voice full
of woe, choking and trembling, cry out,
"Merciful father in heaven, why hast thou
thus punished me?"   I could bear the
sight no longer, and turning, rushed wildly down the avenue, mentally saying,
"Can such grief, so pure, so deep and so
mournful, be mortal?"

Day and night I worked, and as I sat
before the unfinished portrait, that tear-
ful face seemed to haunt me as a vision of
some dream.   How I longed for skill to
make it speak those pleading words which
constantly rang in my ears, " Merciful
father ! why hast thou thus punished me?"
Often as I sat and gazed upon the silent,
speechless picture, I almost fancied she
was near me.

Weeks went by and still I toiled, till
late one night, with aching hands and

throbbing brain I laid my brush aside. The last bit of paint was placed upon the canvas, and I viewed the work of many weary hours finished at last. During all this time I never once inquired, even of myself, who was this strange creature that preyed so upon my mind ; and as I now looked upon her portait, a yearning to see her again, to speak to her, to tell her that, though all the world seemed to turn from her, I alone would pity and aid her in the hour of distress, took posession of me. I fancied I could see her wandering, lonely, and friendless, through the world, with no one to whom she could turn for a word of comfort. My thoughts seem to crowd through my mind, till bewildered and impotent I sank upon the little sofa crying, *"My God, can this be pity or is it love!"*

For weeks I seached the city ; day after day I wandered through the cemetery, hoping chance would again guide me to her side. To hoped seemed vain, to search seemed folly. I endeavored to forget her, but returning to my studio her portrait recalled the scenes I tried so hard to drive from my mind ; and in despair I sent the picture to my parents, instructing them to preserve it till I could look upon it without a thought of the past. Time rolled on, and even now, after ten long, weary years, I can see that face in all its sorrow, as it creeps into my memory, while a voice so low, so sweet and yet so mournful, tinkles into my ear those sad words, " Father in heaven ! why hast thou thus punished me !"